Groundwood Books / House of Anansi Press
groundwoodbooks.com

We gratefully acknowledge for their financial support of our
publishing program the Canada Council for the Arts, the Ontario
Arts Council and the Government of Canada.

Canada Council   Conseil des Arts
for the Arts   du Canada

ONTARIO ARTS COUNCIL
CONSEIL DES ARTS DE L'ONTARIO
an Ontario government agency
un organisme du gouvernement de l'Ontario

With the participation of the Government of Canada   Canadä
Avec la participation du gouvernement du Canada

Library and Archives Canada Cataloguing in Publication
Title: The three brothers / Marie-Louise Gay.
Names: Gay, Marie-Louise, author, illustrator.
Identifiers: Canadiana 20190223731 |
ISBN 9781773063775 (hardcover)
Classification: LCC PS8563.A868 T57 2020 |
DDC jC813/.54—dc23

The illustrations were done in watercolor, pencil, colored pencils,
water-soluble wax crayons and opaque white ink.
Design by Michael Solomon
Printed and bound in China

FSC
www.fsc.org
MIX
Paper from
responsible sources
FSC® C144853

To Virginie E.

THE THREE BROTHERS

MARIE-LOUISE GAY

 Groundwood Books House of Anansi Press Toronto Berkeley

Every night, Finn reads a story to his brothers.
The three brothers love adventure stories about animals
living in dark forests, on top of high mountains
or deep in the jungle.
"When I grow up," said Finn, "I want to be an explorer.
I want to travel around the world to see wild animals."
"Me too," said Leo, the middle brother. "But why wait?
We could go on an expedition tomorrow."
"Yes!" said Finn. "Maybe we will see a bear … or a fox …
or even a wolf!"
"A wolf!" said Leo. "Imagine seeing a wolf!"
Ooley, the smallest brother, just snored.
He always fell asleep before the end of the story.

The three brothers woke up at dawn.
They jumped into their clothes.
They packed their lunches.
They didn't forget the binoculars or the compass.
Finn opened the door. It had snowed all night.
"Uh-oh," said Leo.

The three brothers had to climb out the window.
They didn't have snowshoes,
so they tied pie plates to their boots.
"Follow me," said Finn.

Off they went,
across snowy fields,
up the hill and into the forest.
Ooley had insisted
on wearing his bear suit.
He walked sloooowly
like a bear, swaying
from side to side.
"Wait for me," he said,
in a growly bear voice.

They walked and walked, weaving between the trees,
jumping over logs and falling in the deep, heavy snow.
"Are we there yet?" growled Ooley for the third time.
"Stop talking," said Finn. "You'll scare all the wild animals away."
"What animals?" asked Leo. "I've seen some birds but not one
single wild animal."

"Wait!" said Finn. "Did you hear that?"

Finn stopped. Leo bumped into Finn. Ooley bumped into Leo.

Ooley fell flat on his back like a furry turtle.

"I don't hear anything," said Leo, as he pulled Ooley up.

The forest was still and empty. You could almost hear a snowflake fall.

"I thought I heard a growl," said Finn, "… or a howl … I know there are some animals around. I can almost see them. Can't you?"

Leo shrugged. They trudged on through the snow.

"Wait for meeee!" howled Ooley.

The three brothers finally reached the top of the hill.
They could see the whole world from up there.
"Do you remember Grandpa told us that when he was small
there were hundreds of wild animals in the forest?" asked Finn.
"Yes! He said he saw foxes and bears and badgers and rabbits," said Leo.
"… and chimpunks!" yelled Ooley. "Grandpa saw giant, ferocious
chimpunks!"
"I think he means chipmunks," whispered Finn to Leo.

"But where did the animals go?" asked Leo. "They didn't vanish into thin air."

"Grandpa said that the weather isn't like it used to be," answered Finn. "Sometimes, there are hurricanes or floods. Other times, it is so hot and dry that the forests burn. The animals have to leave their homes to find food and water."

"But here it is cold and snowy," said Leo, "and when spring comes, the snow will melt. There will be water, and berries and mushrooms to eat. Will the animals come back then?"

"I don't know," said Finn. "Grandpa said that people are trying to fix the weather."

"How will they do that?" asked Leo. "Nobody can switch off the sun … or stop the ocean from flooding."

"I don't know, but there must be a way," said Finn.

"Hey! Where's Ooley?" asked Leo.

"He was here a minute ago," said Finn. "Uh-oh … look!"

Leo and Finn stared at the two sets of pie-plate tracks behind them.

O-O-O-O-O-O-L-EY!

The two brothers tramped back and forth between the trees
searching for Ooley.
They called and called.
"O-o-o-ley! O-o-o-o-ley! O-o-o-o-o-o-o-o-o-ley!!!"
The forest echoed back, "O-o-o-o-o-o-o-o-o-ley!"

O·O·O·O·L·E·Y!

It took a long time, but Leo finally found Ooley.
He was in the hollowed-out trunk of the biggest tree in the forest.
"Ooley!" said Leo. "What are you doing in there?"
"This is my bear cave," growled Ooley. "I am going to sleep here until spring, and then I'll come out to eat some berries."

It was the perfect place for a sleepy bear and two cold explorers.
Warm and dry, with piles of soft leaves to sleep on.
It was also a good place to eat lunch.
The three brothers wolfed down their sandwiches.
Finn sighed, "I wish we had seen at least one wild animal."
Leo stared out at the forest.
If we can't see any animals, he thought, why not make some?

And that is what they did …
The three brothers rolled huge snowballs and found
sticks and leaves to make all sorts of animals. A fox
or two, a porcupine, a family of rabbits …

... and an enormous sleeping snow bear.

The moon came up. The herd of wild snow animals
glittered in the silvery light.
"They almost look real," whispered Finn.
"Let's come back with Grandpa tomorrow," said Leo,
as they made their way home. "He can help us make
more animals."
"Grandpa can wear my bear suit," said Ooley,
"if he is too cold."